Burton and Stanley

Burton and Stanley

FRANK O'ROURKE

Pictures by JONATHAN ALLEN

A Sunburst Book

Farrar, Straus and Giroux

*The author wishes to acknowledge
the invaluable help of Ray Quinn,
old friend and master railroader.*

Text copyright © 1993 by Edith Carlson O'Rourke
Pictures copyright © 1993 by Jonathan Allen
All rights reserved
First published in 1993 by David R. Godine, Publisher, Inc.
Published in Canada by HarperCollins*CanadaLtd*
Library of Congress catalog card number: 96-67486
Printed in the United States of America
Sunburst edition, 1996

To Bill Goodman and Audrey Bryant and
David Godine

"The right place,"
chanted the blackbirds.
"At long last, the right place!"

Burton and Stanley

' I '

Mr. Kraft was the Cherrygrove depot agent on the branch line of the Chicago & Northwestern Railroad which ran between Soo City and Bent Fork. One bright morning in September, in 1935, he opened the depot for business at the usual time, half an hour before arrival of the eastbound passenger train. He raised the windows, turned the sounder up on the telegraph, and called, "OM - OM - OM." Omaha answered, "ii - ii - OM," and Mr. Kraft sent the figure 5, which meant "Anything for me?" Omaha replied, "C - L - R," meaning "Clear," and Mr. Kraft continued his morning routine.

He opened the safe, sorted the petty cash into the till under the ticket counter, and glanced at the Seth Thomas clock on the west wall above his rolltop desk.

He went through the inner door into the freight room, pulled the express truck onto the red-brick platform, parked it parallel to the track, and fastened the lock chain on the right rear wheel. He returned to the office, sat at the telegrapher's desk, and began his bookwork.

He typed reports and checked his books, all the while listening automatically to the chatter of the telegraph key as other stations along the branch line started their day. At 7:28 A.M. he heard the iron-tire rasp of the two-wheeled mail cart pushed by the Cherrygrove postmaster. Mr. Kraft donned his ancient Panama hat, gave the saggy crown a pat, and sallied forth. As he left the office his ear caught an odd clicking sound from the vicinity of the telegraph key. There was no time to investigate the minor discord. Mr. Kraft joined his old friend on the platform.

"Good morning, Mr. Bauman."

"Good morning, Mr. Kraft."

The eastbound passenger pulled into Cherrygrove at ten seconds of 7:30 A.M. and stopped with the open door of the railroad post office car exactly in front of them. The chief clerk handed down the incoming mail sacks, took the outgoing sacks from the postmaster, and leaned on the door bar. "No express today, Mr. Kraft," he said, and in the same breath, "Now *there* are the ugliest birds I have ever seen."

"What birds?" Mr. Kraft asked.

"On your depot roof. What are they? You're the bird expert on this line."

Mr. Kraft turned and looked up. His eyes refused to

believe the sight, while his memory frantically flipped the pages of all the bird books he had studied. He reached the only logical conclusion:

"Impossible!"

The conductor called, "All aboard!"

The engineer rang the bell and blew steam; the train moved out with ponderous dignity. The chief postal clerk yanked his blue visor, cupped his hands, and called back: "What did you say they were, Mr. Kraft?"

Mr. Kraft was mumbling to himself, ". . . six, no, more like seven thousand miles!"

"To where?" asked the postmaster, staring at the

two birds leaning against opposite sides of the chimney on the depot roof.

They were big birds, wildly disheveled and preposterously ugly. Their backs, wings, and tails were dirty gray, their long, lumpily jointed legs were dirtier, their underparts were apologetically white, and their necks and heads were an atrocious pink, with truly disagreeable pouches dangling from their throats. Their beady eyes glared at the postmaster and their long, powerful-looking bills clicked in what appeared to be a kind of wordless conversation. Bald heads, untidy feathers, ugly pouches — what unfortunate birds!

The postmaster repeated his question, "To where, Mr. Kraft?"

"East Equatorial Africa, Mr. Bauman! They'd have to cross that continent, the Atlantic Ocean, the Gulf of Mexico, fly up the Mississippi River Valley, then the Missouri. Impossible!"

"What are they, Mr. Kraft?"

"Unless I am mistaken, they are marabou storks."

The postmaster ventured a humanitarian observation: "They look tired and hungry. What do they eat?"

"Fish, mollusks, frogs, snakes, insects, carrion."

"Carrion?"

"They are scavengers, Mr. Bauman, valuable assets in their native communities."

"How big are they?"

"They grow four feet high."

"What's their wingspan?"

"Six to eight feet."

The postmaster whistled. He wanted to ask more

questions, but he had to distribute the mail before his customers became impatient.

"Got to get cracking, Mr. Kraft. Call me if you need me."

"Thank you, Mr. Bauman, I will."

Alone, Mr. Kraft tried to analyze the situation: had a freak storm of unimaginable strength sprung up around the cloud-swept, snow-covered heights of Mount Kilimanjaro, caught the two storks in its blustery grasp, and hurled them westward until, on this fall morning, they found themselves in Cherrygrove?

"Bosh!" he said sheepishly.

There had to be a logical explanation, and being a logical man, Mr. Kraft supplied it: the storks had escaped from a zoo aviary. He would telegraph the proper authorities and report the incident when he finished his morning bookwork. Satisfied with his solution, he went inside and resumed his morning schedule.

He had scarcely settled into the chair at the telegrapher's desk when he heard that strange clicking sound again. It was coming down through the open windows from the depot roof. Belatedly, he remembered that storks, like vultures and buzzards, had no syrinx muscles. They were mute, but produced a clattering sound by snapping their bills. He smiled in smug satisfaction of another logical explanation which, to his horror, collapsed around him. The sound of the stork bills suddenly turned into a string of Morse code!

"Burton, this is not Jinja Station."

"It is not, Stanley."

"Nor is this the Kenya-Uganda Railway."

"Stanley, where are we?"

"I am at a loss, Burton."

Acting without conscious volition, Mr. Kraft's hand tapped the closed telegraph key: "Cherrygrove, branch line, Chicago & Northwestern Railroad."

Silence poured down eloquently from overhead. Then a bill snapped tentatively, "Who sent that?"

"Kraft, Cherrygrove depot agent."

"What colonial district?"

Mr. Kraft summoned up all his African knowledge and tried to match American geographical divisions to Kenya. "Not called colonial districts, they are called states."

"What country?"

"U.S.A."

8

The other bill clicked, "Do you believe him, Burton?"

"Stanley, have we a choice?"

Mr. Kraft was cursed with an orderly mind and blessed with a vivid imagination. All his adult life had been spent judiciously suppressing that imagination, never allowing himself more than one dream a day. But time and life had finally caught him. He had gone round the bend, off the rails, down the chute. If the storks on the depot roof were bewildered and frightened, what about him? Humans were supposedly the only species on earth capable of reason, always calm and clear-headed even when thrown willy-nilly into hurricanes, typhoons, earthquakes, fire, war, peace, and other dreadful calamities. He took a trembling grip on his sensibility and tapped out a discreet question:

"Are you hungry, thirsty?"

"Excessively."

"West along the track — "

"Rails?"

"Called track here — " Mr. Kraft began falling into the time-saving method employed by all Morse code operators, that of eliminating unnecessary words, " — as was sending, quarter-mile west, second bridge crosses a slough — "

"A what?"

"Excuse — marsh."

"Understood — water, food?"

"Yes."

"Can you fly, Burton?"

"Stanley, one must try."

Mr. Kraft heard the scrape of talons on the depot roof, followed by the swish of heavy wings. He looked out the west bay window and saw the storks flying low above the railroad track toward the slough. Mr. Kraft wondered what would happen if he walked across the switch track into the lumberyard owned by his friend Pat Brown and said off-handedly, "Been talking in Morse code with a pair of marabou storks from Africa." Pat Brown would say, "Now just take it easy, Franklin," and the next thing Mr. Kraft knew, he would be gracing a padded cell in the Bent Fork Insane Asylum. And he could not blame Pat Brown for believing that he had gone stark, raving mad. He had to think this business through and the best way to begin was to finish his morning work, so he did, checking everything twice before he sat back in his chair and gave himself over to a calming fit of nerves.

Familiar Cherrygrove sounds filtered soothingly through the open windows, filling the office with that soft persuasion that made people settle comfortably into the ruts of daily life. Voices, footsteps, wind in the trees, sunlight on the leaves. Time for dreaming. But the dreams of that gay blade Franklin Kraft, gallantly rescuing fair maidens, dueling villains, climbing castle walls, did not materialize. An unimaginable dream had just come true. Had it found him wanting? Did he have the courage to rise to the occasion, to quench the raging fire, parry cold steel, rescue the fair maiden? Or was he doubting the dream? Was he finding it hard to believe?

He was roused from his reverie by the sound of talons

on the roof; the storks had returned from the slough. Mr. Kraft returned to reality — or was it the other way around. He tapped:

"Feel better?"

"Much, thank you."

Mr. Kraft identified the sender's style. "Burton?"

The bill snapped, "You recognize quickly."

"Your fist — " Mr. Kraft corrected himself, " — your bill tighter than Stanley's."

"True," Stanley chimed in. "Yours clean, clear."

"Thank you," Mr. Kraft replied, and then, overcome with curiosity, "What happened Africa?"

"Stanley, do honors."

"Will try," Stanley began. "We residents Jinja Station, Kenya-Uganda Protectorate, main line Kenya-Uganda Railway, ab-officio employees Public Health Service, charged keeping main line clear and sanitary, east west Jinja Station. Continue, Burton, I am still parched."

Burton's tighter bill took up the tale. "Some days ago, four miles east Jinja Station, reducing remains of cow struck previous week by night goods train. Hot day, dark clouds developed, extended downward, created rotating black column — "

"Funnel-shaped?" Mr. Kraft interjected.

"Yes."

"Here called tornado, cyclone, twister."

"Apt name. Funnel swallowed us, hurled skyward, expelled in fading light, had brief glimpse Kilimanjaro lower left rear before blown west on fierce horizontal wind. Helpless to escape. Set wings, soared, glided,

breathing difficult. Resume, Stanley, bill hurts."

"Sun rose our rear," Stanley clicked. "Water below to all horizons. Wind blew us westward all day, night, another day. Saw islands, wind shifted southeast, blew us northwest through night, dawn above great river valley. Wind shifted sunset, blew us west, then north, up second great river. Carry on, Burton."

"Late night," Burton continued. "Exhausted, hungry, thirsty. Wind dropped, flew downward, end of endurance when we saw lights, alit on station roof. You found us. We throw ourselves on your benevolent grace."

Mr. Kraft believed that Burton's words were the most felicitous ever spoken to him. Dare he respond in less generous fashion? He tried to restore their confidence:

"Suggest you rest, sleep, become accustomed to new surroundings."

✶   ✶   ✶

There are red-letter days and black-armband days and gray humdrum days. That sunny day could have been thumbtacked on the solar spectrum scale as star spangled. All the residents of Cherrygrove visited the depot to see the storks and ask the same questions twenty times over. Mr. Kraft did not mind answering the kindly curious, but he disliked those people who saw the storks as unwelcome intruders. The banker's wife was the most voluble.

"Disgusting!"

Pat Brown said, "What is?"

Mrs. Thurber was a woman who demanded the moon at noon; unfortunately, the only man capable of obliging her lived on the moon. She looked up at the storks and wrinkled her frosty nose.

"Are you going to let them stay in town?"

"They're lost," Pat Brown said. "They need help."

"They'd better find themselves — " Mrs. Thurber recalled a scrap of forgotten fashion lore, " — didn't they make boa scarves from stork feathers?"

"Yes," Mr. Kraft said. "Marabou underfeathers are very soft."

"Fancy that," Mrs. Thurber sniffed. "Who would guess there's anything pretty about such dirty, ugly birds."

"They always looked ugly to me," Mr. Kraft said mildly. "The people who wore the scarves, I mean, not the scarves."

"Humph!" Mrs. Thurber said, and marched uptown to tell her husband that the depot agent was getting uppity again. Mr. Thurber persuaded her to go home, and sighed as he returned to his desk. He could not concentrate on business, so he clapped his hat on his bald head and walked down to the depot.

"Where are the storks?"

"Just flew out to the slough," Pat Brown said. "Sit down, take the weight off your mind."

Mr. Thurber sat beside Pat Brown and Mr. Kraft on the edge of the red-brick platform and put his shoes on the inside rail, the way he had sat barefooted in his Iowa hometown fifty years ago when the world was a good deal brighter. During a hiatus of visitors and trains, the three friends talked quietly about the storks and the weather and if enough rain would fall to break the drouth. They were recalling the unexpected juiciness of elderberry pies three seasons ago when the children came running from school at the same moment the storks came flying back from the slough. Men and children watched the storks circle the depot and land on the roof. Mr. Thurber whistled with the amazement of the small boy he had been hiding inside his blue serge vest for the past half hour.

"I see what you mean. You're darn tootin' we've got to help them. Count me in."

"Knew we could," Pat Brown smiled. "We'll keep you posted, Estel."

"You do that — " Mr. Thurber took a last look at the storks, " — well, back to the interest tables."

"Me too," Pat Brown said. "See you both at board meeting tonight."

Mr. Kraft started into the depot, but found himself surrounded by children. Now came all the delightful, impractical questions: did the legs always dangle when the storks flew, what were the neck pouches for, were they the biggest storks?

"I'm not sure," Mr. Kraft said, "but I'll find out."

"Do they deliver babies?"

"So I've heard."

"How many toes have they got?"

"Can you count them?"

"How many kinds of storks are there?"

Mr. Kraft tried to remember: saddle-billed, white

and black, jabiru, adjutant, and the only native North American stork, the wood ibis. He said, "Six or seven."

"What are these?"

"Marabous, members of the adjutant family."

"Why are they called adjutant?"

"Because they stand up straight like soldiers, and strut when they walk."

"Where do they live?"

"East Equatorial Africa."

Finally, questions exhausted, the children scattered homeward. Mr. Kraft went inside, sat at the telegrapher's desk, and tapped:

"All clear."

Burton immediately snapped, "Who man named Estel?"

"Mr. Thurber, banker."

"Who horrid woman?"

"Mrs. Thurber — " Mr. Kraft sat bolt upright, startled and amazed for the second time that day. "Did not send name, spoke it on platform. You understand our speech!"

"Yes."

"When did you learn?"

"Folklore says 1901," Stanley clicked. "Year Kenya-Uganda Railway completed. Ancestors settled Jinja Station, watched stationmaster, listened, by time we born, understood code, speech."

"How?"

"Cannot explain, just can."

Mr. Kraft had another thought, really a secret belief he had nursed for years. "Can you communicate with other birds?"

"Yes."

"With bills, hisses?"

"No."

"Thought?"

"In best sense," Stanley clicked. "Spoonbill once said all birds like seashells, hear echoes of time."

Mr. Kraft sat at the telegrapher's desk in the twilight, watching time fall off the clock. He heard tonight's echoes following today's into the stillness of yesterday. He tapped, "Understood."

"You are one with us."

Mr. Kraft experienced a humble feeling of discovery long felt in his bones.

‵ **2** ′

The storks flew out to the slough at sunrise, to eat, drink, and question the red-winged blackbirds who had given them a warm welcome the previous day. The blackbirds were entranced by the storks. They perched on the swaying cattails and answered questions while the storks fished for frogs, crawdads, minnows, and snakes. They assured the storks that no dangerous animals lurked beyond the fringe of plum brush and willows ringing the slough, but warned that a deadly enemy was rapidly approaching. The storks looked up in alarm.

"Deadly enemy?"

"Winter."

"How cold does it get?"

"Unspeakable! Almost all birds go south."

The storks stood rigid as petrified soldiers, watching the tiny water bugs skate across the placid surface of the water. The wind was cool, the sun shone beneficently, hunting was good. How could this climatic prospect wane? They walked stiff-legged from the water and began hunting mice and grasshoppers in the tall grass. The blackbirds fluttered around them, balancing gracefully on the long grass blades. The storks swallowed their fear and faced the danger.

"How can we go south?"

The blackbirds rose up in a cloud of flashing wings and made a complete circuit of the slough, a tactic that gave them time to think. The blackbirds loved to tell stories in which the entire flock participated, each member adding a line to the tale in the fashion of wandering troubadors singing for their supper. They settled down around the storks and began a communal prose poem. From the tiptop of a willow came the liquid voice of a sentry:

"See the slough?"

"See the creek beyond the track?" shrilled an old-timer.

"Spring Creek," trilled a young matron under Burton's tail, and one sang after another, their shining, opalescent throats sliding beads onto the poetic necklace:

"Spring Creek flows into the river."

"The Bent Fork River."

"Which flows south into the Buckhorn River."

"Which flows east and south into the Platte River."

"Which flows east into the Missouri River."

"Which flows south and east into the Mississippi River."

"Which flows south into the Gulf of Mexico."

"Which blends into the Caribbean Sea."

"Which streams into the Atlantic Ocean."

"Which is good luck for you."

The storks appreciated the geography lesson but, "Who will guide us?"

"The long-distance fliers will lend a wing."

A sentry on the near telegraph pole announced the imminent arrival of the morning passenger. The storks bade the blackbirds good morning and flew back to the depot, where Mr. Kraft and the postmaster stood in the same spot on the platform. The storks lit beside the chimney, folded their wings, and watched yesterday's scene repeat itself. The train moved out, the postmaster trundled his mail cart uptown, and Mr. Kraft went into the office. A minute later came his opening tap.

"Good morning."

"Good morning, Mr. Kraft."

"Sleep well?"

"Yes, thank you."

The storks fell silent. Mr. Kraft had the feeling they were trying to phrase a delicate statement, and he was equally certain it would be forthcoming only after they, in the manner of most humans, chose to dissemble before speaking hard truth. Stanley finally clicked:

"Have personal problem."

"Please explain."

"Slough water does not agree with stomachs."

"Alkali."

"Yes. Blackbirds say try windmill tanks."

"Excellent idea," Mr. Kraft agreed. "May I suggest alternative? Cherrygrove town well pumps pure, cold water. Can place small trough west side depot, fill from faucet. Convenient, safe."

The storks snapped and clicked approval, and then, as Mr. Kraft had guessed, approached their real problem. Burton snapped:

"Argued all night, must tell why."

"Please do."

". . . do not misunderstand . . . find Cherrygrove fascinating."

"Good."

"Eager explore countryside."

"You must."

"Can see, learn much."

"You will."

"But must face greater truth . . ."

Mr. Kraft tapped, "You want to go home."

"Yes!" the storks snapped enthusiastically.

Mr. Kraft knew that people ought to change their lives to fit their changing times and circumstances, but the storks had not found a better way of life, just a different life. Besides, if you could not drink the local water, you were in a bad way. He was honor-bound to help them find their way home, so they could fit themselves back into their own time and life. He tapped:

"What is worst obstacle to return, in your minds?"

Burton answered, "Cannot fly Atlantic Ocean."

"Combine problems — go south for winter, find way to cross ocean."

The storks' reply sagged with doubt. "But how?"

"Have idea," Mr. Kraft tapped. "Need time."

Their relief was palpable. "You believe possible?"

"Yes."

Mr. Kraft heard their talons scratch the roof in an ecstasy of restored confidence. They did not ask what his idea was. They trusted him. He tapped a final message before returning to his work.

"Offer suggestion — you must pass time."

"Yes."

"See Cherrygrove, surrounding country."

"Will do."

The storks regained lost strength as, escorted by the blackbirds, they flew tourist circles around Cherry-grove but they did not venture farther than a mile from the depot. Mr. Kraft took them to task.

"Fly higher."

Burton snapped, "To see what?"

"The next horizon."

"Another circle, hemming us in."

"Could be a signpost, leading to freedom."

"Freedom from what?"

Mr. Kraft persisted. He wanted to jiggle them, joggle and foggle them, make them eager to dare the unknown.

"Meeting other birds?"

"Yes."

"Like them?"

"Kind, friendly, helpful."

Mr. Kraft asked them which birds they liked best.

"Blackbirds, little meadowlark — "

"Dickcissels," Mr. Kraft tapped. "Happy singers."

The storks agreed that the dickcissels *were* happy singers. They told of meeting a pair of rose-breasted grosbeaks, several wrens and finches, and a sparrow named Harris. Growing more confident, they widened their circle of exploration and then, on Tuesday, October 1st, they returned early in complete disarray. Mr. Kraft tapped:

"What happened?"

"Shot at."

"Where?"

"North three miles, farm with green barn."

"I know the farm," Mr. Kraft tapped. "Was it little boy with gun that went ping?"

"Yes, small boy."

"Beebee gun," Mr. Kraft tapped. "Not dangerous unless hit in eye. Father teaching boy shoot."

Irony dripped from Burton's bill. "Fly higher! See next horizon!"

"Should have warned you," Mr. Kraft tapped. "Must always be wary guns."

Stanley clicked, "Why they shoot?"

Mr. Kraft had several easy answers on the tip of his telegraph key, but he did not trust easy answers. He searched his mind for words that explained why some humans seemed to find enjoyment in shooting birds and animals; yes, and shooting other human beings. He tried to describe an ancient, cave-dwelling instinct. He tapped:

"Do not know why, unless their thoughts so ugly they cannot bear see beauty live in anything else."

The storks shuffled nervously and tried to remain calm. The children were a great help that afternoon. They had gotten into the pleasant habit of stopping by the depot after school, with tidbits for the storks and fresh questions for Mr. Kraft. They asked more than their ordinary number of questions, and offered the storks some truly exotic food. Sugar cookies, peppermint sticks, dried peas, navy beans, and from Molly Green, the uneaten half of her Eskimo pie. The children laid their offerings on the depot grass plot, called good-by to the storks and Mr. Kraft, and went their

varied ways. Stanley considered the treasure trove and
questioned,

"Eskimo pie?"

Mr. Kraft smiled. "Chocolate-covered ice cream."

The storks flew down on the grass, laid their bills
alongside the Eskimo pie, and chopped off side pieces.
They nibbled gingerly, swallowed, and hissed. Mr.
Kraft tapped, "Like it?"

"Cannot say."

Next morning the blackbirds led the storks west to
a small lake where they fished, met a flock of coot,
and returned with revived spirits. Mr. Kraft tapped,

"Red-letter day!" and reported that his idea was working. He had requested help from his colleagues in the Gulf Coast area concerning the departure of ships for the west coast of Africa, and dozens of generous agents and operators were compiling a master list, with the names of captains willing to carry two marabou storks. Burton immediately snapped,

"Far-fetched."

"Not so," Mr. Kraft rebutted. "Ships sail weekly Africa."

"Ships sail, how many captains willing carry storks?"

"Be surprised," Mr. Kraft tapped, and came at last to the heart and soul of his plan. "You must ask birds for escort. Have birds lead you south, board ship, sail safely for Africa."

Burton snapped, "Serious flaw."

"Am aware," Mr. Kraft admitted. "Captain and crew watch two storks fly from sky, board ship, ask how storks knew ship?"

"Yes — how explain?"

"Do not explain. Trust, have faith."

"So you said before!"

"Have you better idea?"

Burton was silent. Stanley clicked. "We apologize. You offer life, we act ungrateful. Time to cooperate."

The storks did not wait for morning, but flew back to the slough and explained everything to the blackbirds. The blackbirds said, "We need the crows," and led the storks south to the canyon in the big cow pasture where they met the local flock. The crows held

28

a caucus and sent their strongest young fliers north to the Chalk Bluff crows on the Missouri River. The Chalk Bluff crows would dispatch their scouts to contact the first migrating ducks and geese along the Souris River.

Waiting for news from the north, the storks paced the depot roof, pestered Mr. Kraft with useless questions, and hiccuped while they fished. The blackbirds tried to soothe them with song and cattail dances, and the crows counseled patience.

"Keep busy," they urged. "Come exploring with us, fly a lot, exercise your wings."

The storks clenched their talons and swallowed the impulse to hiss with frustration. They fished and hunted, played captive audience to the blackbirds, and accompanied the crows on leisurely expeditions to all the compass points. They visited the Bent Fork and Buckhorn Rivers, ranged around Cherrygrove in high, ever-widening circles, watched the farmers pick corn, mend fence, patch holes; saw the children walking to country schools, soon recognized the rural mail carrier's Model A roadster bumping dustily along the section roads. His name, said the crows, was Herb, and all the birds liked him because he waved at them as he passed, as if they were regular customers with their own mail boxes.

The storks usually returned to Cherrygrove in early afternoon, and perched in the schoolhouse bell tower where they could watch, and listen to, the cheerful uproar of the children. At the conclusion of recess they flew to the depot, where, during the quiet hours that

soft-shoed toward suppertime, they held long conversations with Mr. Kraft, and gradually, as the days grew colder and shorter, they ceased to be strangers in a foreign town, felt themselves become a part of the community. Not residents, never more than welcome transients, but accepted, strange faces carved half-familiar by time.

↗ ↗ ↗

On the afternoon of Friday, October 11th, the storks flew such a long reconnoiter with the crows that they did not settle down on the depot roof until minutes before school let out. Mr. Kraft opened the window, jiggled his key, and tapped:

"News from north?"

"Not yet," Stanley clicked. "From Gulf?"

"No, but soon. Feel it in bones."

"Feel cold in bones," Burton snapped. "Ice on slough this morning."

Mr. Kraft injected a note of levity to take their minds off the gravity of avalanching events, foremost of which was the start of hunting season on October 19th. "Know exactly what you need."

Burton snapped, "Miracle?"

"Good fairy tale." And Mr. Kraft began tapping, "Once upon time in country of moon, there were two storks — " yes, Mr. Kraft thought, that was the only way to start a tale of high adventure, " — fine feathered young knights, distant cousins by marriage to their king, dear friends of the king's beautiful daughter, the princess. While the knights were far away on the crusade to free cows in the distant land of Bovinia — "

"Here, here!" clapped the storks.

"Thank you," Mr. Kraft tapped, and rolled on, " — the king's evil brother overthrew and exiled the king, assumed the throne, and ordered the princess to marry his blackhearted henchman named Raven. She refused, and the evil king imprisoned her in the Tower of Tears until she agreed to marry Raven — "

"Never!" Burton snapped, and Stanley echoed, "Never!" and Mr. Kraft began describing the Tower of Tears, but Burton suddenly broke in:

"Truck parking, two men getting out, looking at us, waving arms, excited."

Mr. Kraft tapped, "Stay put!" and hurried from the

depot to meet the two men whose weathered faces creased in practiced smiles as they extended callused hands.

"Johnson," said the tall, thin man who resembled an emaciated sandhill crane. "Naturalist from the State Fish and Game Commission."

"Jackson," said the short, stout man who gave the impression of a bronze Chinese idol left in a pawnshop window until gray dustballs gathered on his fringe of faded brown hair. "State zoo ornithologist."

"Kraft, Cherrygrove depot agent. What can I do to help you?"

Johnson pointed to the storks. "Marabous!"

"Yes."

"We thought it was mistaken identity."

"Come again?"

"About the storks," Jackson said. "We received a letter from Cherrygrove, stating that two marabou storks were roosting on the depot roof, being cared for by the agent and friends. We were asked to remove them to a safe place before winter set in and they froze to death. We felt certain they were ibis, but there they are. It's impossible, but they *are* marabous."

While Jackson was talking, the children came from school, formed a circle around Mr. Kraft and the two men, and listened to the conversation. When they heard Jackson say, " — remove them to a safe place — " they began waving their arms in protest.

Mr. Kraft asked, "Who wrote you?"

"A Mrs. Thurber," Johnson said. "Plainly a bird lover, to be so concerned. Will you help us set up our net?"

"Net?" chorused the children.

"No," said Mr. Kraft.

"But why not?" Johnson asked.

"There's a town ordinance," Mr. Kraft said. "No trapping birds and animals inside the town limits."

33

"But surely," said Jackson, "you will waive the ordinance for humanitarian purposes."

"That's why we passed it," Mr. Kraft said. "For humanitarian purposes."

"What do they want to do, Mr. Kraft?" asked the children.

"They say they want to save the storks from freezing. They want to take them away."

"How?"

"Trap them with nets. You see all the paraphernalia on the truck? Looks like a big minnow net with poles and springs and ropes."

The children stared aghast. "Is that a cage on the truck?"

"Yes," Johnson said. "A portable cage, to carry the storks safely to the zoo."

"What then?" asked the boy who stood near the truck.

"Why," Jackson explained patiently, "they will be cared for in the aviary. Good food and water, the very best care. Have you children visited the zoo, seen the aviary and all the birds? Tell your parents, come visit the storks."

Molly Green looked at Mr. Kraft. "How long will the storks stay in the zoo?"

Mr. Kraft said, "Ask these gentlemen."

Jackson did not tell little white lies. "For the rest of their lives."

"But they want to go home!"

"To Africa?"

"Yes."

Jackson smiled kindly. "How do you know that?"

"We know!" the children shouted with one voice. "We just know! We don't want them shut up. We want them to go home!"

Jackson shook his head in wonder at such dreaming by seemingly sensible children. Johnson said, "Excuse us a minute," and led Jackson to their truck. They stood with their left feet on the running board, forearms on the windowsill, looking exactly like a pair of farmers discussing crops. Mr. Kraft was not fooled. They were dedicated scientists of vast professional and political experience, undismayed by local ordinances, secure in the knowledge that important people in high places would support them, once they explained how valuable the marabou storks were in terms of research and publicity. The end was inevitable: Burton and Stanley trapped, caged, transported to the zoo, freedom forever lost. He heard Johnson say, "Too late today, let's go back to the hotel."

Jackson nodded. They called good-by to Mr. Kraft and the children, got into their truck, backed out, and headed for Bent Fork. The children crowded around Mr. Kraft, still holding the foodstuffs they had brought to tempt the storks. He saw a black licorice stick, and three entwined strands of spaghetti — pasta for a stork! How the world needed their natural compassion.

"Mr. Kraft," they begged, "don't let them trap the storks!"

"I won't."

"We'll help, just tell us what to do!"

"I will — now it's late, you are all overdue at home."

The children called good-by to the storks, laid their offerings on the grass, and disbanded. Mr. Kraft returned to the office and tapped:

"You heard?"

"Yes," Burton snapped. "Net, cage and poles and — " Burton stopped as his bill gnashed in rage.

"Yes," Mr. Kraft tapped. "All used in trapping."

"Bad men," Stanley clicked. "Very bad!"

"Doing their job," Mr. Kraft tapped. "No evil intent."

"Result evil," Burton snapped.

"True, in sense."

"We'll stay in town."

"You must fish, hunt," Mr. Kraft reminded them. "Keep up strength. Most important, fly every day, exercise wings for long flight south. Ask crows put scouts on Bent Fork highway, watch for truck approach. Be doubly cautious. Fly high, maintain room maneuver, escape net."

' 3 '

Early Saturday morning, Johnson and Jackson parked their Fish and Game Commission truck on the highway curve overlooking the slough, uncased binoculars, and watched the storks fish. The black-birds and crows kept them under constant surveillance and they made no suspicious moves, but after the storks flew back to the depot, they began a crisscrossing search of the countryside, driving the square-mile grids of section road. The crows reported their every move from Saturday morning until Sunday night, and Burton's first question on Monday morning was:

"What they up to?"

"Picking best spot trap you," Mr. Kraft replied. Mr. Kraft tapped that if he were planning it, he'd bring in more Fish and Game Commission men, drive the

crows from the canyon, and hide a spring net in the loose brown sand under the big dead tree, baited with the finest well-cured meat. When the storks saw and smelled such aromatic food, how could they resist spiraling down for a good meal? At their first eager, vigorous bites, the triggers would pop, the springs jump, the poles leap up and over, covering the storks with layers of netting. And that, he reminded them, was only one trap in the least-expected place; others could, and would, be set in the slough and along the shores of the lake.

"Please believe me," Mr. Kraft concluded. "Can happen unless you very careful."

The storks scratched the roof in an agony of apprehension. Stanley clicked, "Should start south now."

"Cannot. You must wait word from geese."

"Crows promise tomorrow." Mr. Kraft could feel the worry in Burton's snap. "What your word from Gulf Coast?"

Mr. Kraft tapped, "Nothing yet," and then he had to tell them about the worst danger. "Hunting season opens Saturday morning, October 19th. You should start south two days earlier, stay ahead of guns."

"Thursday?" they cracked in alarm. "Only three days!"

"Absolute limit Friday morning. News or no news, you must go."

"Fly blind?" Stanley clicked. "No ship name, no port, where to board?"

"Better than guns . . . please, we should not argue."

Mr. Kraft closed the window and began the morning work. He needed to bolster his own courage, and wasn't it odd that he had never doubted the storks, no matter their momentary pips and palpitations? He knew why. Their world was harsher than his.

✐　✐　✐

The storks maintained their routine through an uneventful day. Tuesday morning brought no news from north *or* south; and just as Mr. Kraft suspected, Johnson and Jackson finished their extensive exploration and took action. The storks flew out to the slough, to fish and hunt, and found men setting up pole nets and rowing boats that muddied the crystal-clear water; then crow scouts brought word that more men had driven the flock from the canyon. As Tuesday wore on, blackbirds and crows discovered men at the lake, along Spring Creek, and near all roosting places. Late in the afternoon, Mr. Kraft assessed the gathered information and ventured an opinion:

"Making all good spots impossible to use."

"What do?" Burton asked.

Tomorrow was Wednesday; hope was dying in Mr. Kraft's heart. He could not see the storks on the roof, but he knew that part of that indomitable, sometimes arrogant gleam in their eyes was dulled. They were starting to droop, and their bills did not crack with the usual crispness. He tapped, "Stay on roof, sleep," and hurried home to do the last thing he could think of: open his atlases and reference books, list all information available about the Port of New Orleans and the Mississippi delta. The most he could do was tell them where to fly, what to look for, and how to continue southward to tropical lands if necessary.

At midnight he closed the books and went to bed. Instead of sheep, he counted one small satisfaction: he, the storks, the crows and blackbirds, and the town ordinance — all had combined to neutralize the best efforts of Johnson and Jackson, and preserve the storks' freedom. He slept fitfully and walked to the depot Wednesday morning, prepared for the worst. He received the best.

✓ ✓ ✓

The long, detailed message had come up the Mississippi Valley from New Orleans over a dozen railroad lines, deliberately sent back and forth, up and down, to and fro, so that prying ears and traitorous eyes could not intercept the vital information. Mr. Kraft's fellow agents and operators on the Santa Fe, the Southern Pacific, the Katy, the Frisco, the Missouri Pacific, the Louisiana Southern, the Burlington, the C & NW had done yeoman work. Mr. Kraft took it all down, read it twice, and felt like dancing. He opened the window and tapped:

"Good morning, gentlemen."

He could taste the gloom in Stanley's reply, "Good morning, Mr. Kraft."

"News from south."

Mr. Kraft tapped the magic words so casually that no reply came for a dozen heartbeats, then he heard the talons on the roof as his meaning shattered their apathy. Burton snapped,

"Have ship?"

"*Glad Tidings*, Captain Littlefield out of Portland, Maine, loading assorted cargo Port of New Orleans, bound for Caribbean, South America, Africa, Europe."

Stanley's bill rattled in a jig of happy consonants and billables. "Captain willing take us?"

"Waiting welcome you aboard."

"When sail?"

"October 29th. Will make port, unload cargo, Kingston, Willemstad, Belém, Santos, Montevideo, Buenos Aires. Will load large cargo dried beef in Buenos Aires — "

Burton snapped, "Dried beef?"

Mr. Kraft smiled. "For Bristol. But from Buenos Aires, cross Atlantic, unload last machinery Lobito, Portuguese West Africa. You leave ship there, follow railroad east and north to Katanga, Northern Rhodesia,

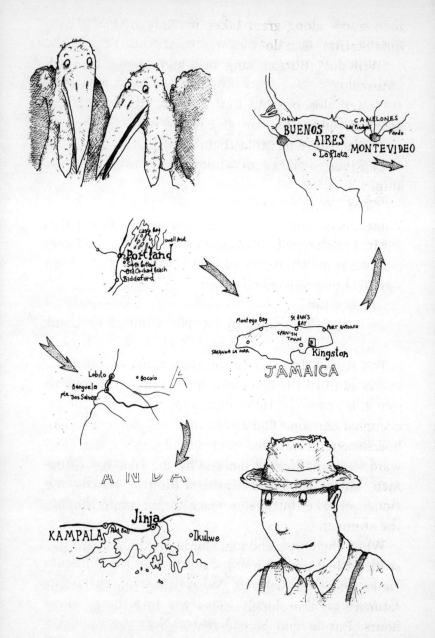

then north along great lakes to Tanganyika, Kenya, Jinja Station. Can do?"

"Will do!" Burton sang out, and Stanley echoed, "Must do!"

"Listen closely," Mr. Kraft tapped. "Last night prepared directions for you, in case no news from north . . . " and Mr. Kraft told them how to fly the Mississippi River to the delta where they would meet the ship.

"*Glad Tidings*," Stanley clicked. "Has good sound. What means?"

Mr. Kraft tapped, "In Gospel according to St. Luke, text suggests phrase employed by Angel Gabriel as sign of hope and good news in troubled world."

✝   ✝   ✝

The storks flew out to the slough and circled high overhead until the blackbirds joined them; all flew to join the crows in their makeshift roost east of the occupied canyon. The crows received the news with hoarse congratulations, and led the hungry storks eastward to a small creek ignored by the Fish and Game men, not as good a fishing and hunting spot as the slough or lake, but a safe place to put something on the stomach.

While the crows and blackbirds mounted guard, the storks fished the little holes and hunted on the shady banks under the willows. Noon came; the blackbirds returned to the slough, expecting to be gone three hours. But lo and behold! they came rushing back within the hour, leading a pair of weary scouts just arrived from the Chalk Bluff crows on the Missouri River.

"News!" the blackbirds shouted. "Wonderful news!"

The Chalk Bluff scouts reported that a pathfinder flight of Canada geese had reached the bluffs and even now were feeding in the adjacent fields. They would fly over the Cherrygrove depot at dawn, and they sent a short, succinct message: "Be ready when we call!"

"A small V," the Chalk Bluff scouts told the storks. "Young, strong, full of ginger! They will circle the depot twice, you must fly up and join them on their third circle because they will not wait."

"Full of ginger!" cried the blackbirds. "Think of that, they will not wait!"

"They know the Gulf Coast," the Chalk Bluff escorts assured the storks. "They know the delta. They will take you straight to the right place."

"The right place," chanted the blackbirds. "At long last, the right place!"

The storks were already flying back to Cherrygrove. The crows and blackbirds followed, all came streaming into town past the standpipe and the bell tower, over the leafless trees under the gray autumn sky that, for no meteorological reason, let the sun shine through. The storks came down on the depot roof with a thump, caught their breath, folded their wings, and rattled their bills like a pair of sabers. The children were coming from school, the sun was shining, and Mr. Kraft, painfully aware of fleeting time, opened the window to hear whatever news the storks had brought.

When Burton snapped, "Geese coming," Mr. Kraft was reborn.

"Tomorrow morning," Stanley clicked. "At dawn. Told us be ready."

"You see!" Mr. Kraft tapped, as though he had seen all along and never entertained a smidgen of doubt. He saw the blackbirds crowding the telegraph wires, the crows sitting on the crossarms, the children staring at the assemblage in open-mouthed surprise. Burton asked, "Shall we fly?"

"In celebration?" Mr. Kraft tapped.

"Yes."

"Then fly!"

Mr. Kraft hurried outside and stood in front of the depot with the children. Pat Brown walked across the switch track from the lumberyard, looked at the blackbirds, and said, "Never knew them to stay so late," and suddenly the crows rose from the crossarms, the blackbirds lifted from the wires and swooped in hubless wheels of shimmering color. As one, storks and crows and blackbirds flew eastward past the elevators above the open fields . . . suddenly out of the westering sun came the biggest bird ever seen in Blackbird County.

Wings glinting in the sunlight, landing gear wheels turning lazily in the slipstream, two leather helmets visible in the side-by-side cabin seats — and what was that suspended beneath the body of the high-winged monoplane? Why, it was a net, the release ropes held by the helmet in the left-hand cabin seat. And who was the man under the helmet? None other than that

canny old ornithologist named Jackson, directing the pilot as the airplane swooped down above the storks, scattering the crows and blackbirds like chaff from a thresher blower, slamming crows this way, blackbirds that, as the pilot cut his motor to stalling speed and for one breathless moment hovered directly above the storks. Jackson gave his ropes a hard pull, the catches opened, the fine-meshed net weighted around the rim with lead slugs belled outward to the gentle holding action of a pocket-sized parachute, billowed into twenty-four feet of imprisonment, and descended over the storks like a circle of doom.

Mr. Kraft saw it all and he thought of pride going after a fall; it was his fault, he should have known. He watched the net fall upon the storks, who appeared frozen in space. The distance between dropping net and storks shrank so rapidly it seemed certain they could not escape — but as the rim of net began cupping inward in the classic trapping movement, the storks folded their wings and dropped like plummets — fifty, feet, one hundred, their wings opened, beat powerfully, they veered off to the south, into clear air, one eye-boggling split-second before the net dropped through their vacated air space and streamed downward onto the ground. The airplane banked and disappeared into the sun, and all the children in front of the depot waved their arms and cheered.

✓   ✓   ✓

In the late fall, sunrise did not come willingly to dispel the darkness. Mr. Kraft had plenty of time on Thursday morning to build fires in the waiting room and office stoves, open the window, and give the telegraph key a little poke as he faced the moment that was sad, and joyful, but mostly full of life as it should be lived. He did not sit at the big desk, but stood above the key and listened to the sounds outside the window. He heard the storks move on the roof, and then he heard a faint, far sound in the north and recognized the haunting, mellow honk of Canada geese coming swiftly on the morning wind. A small pathfinder V, the Chalk Bluff crows had said, a dozen or so big, strong fliers with powerful wings, born to wind and sky and weather. Through the open window he heard their call and watched the sky fade from gray to white, revealing clouds and patches of pale blue. He tapped, "Good morning, Burton. Good morning, Stanley."

"Good morning, Mr. Kraft."

"Sleep well?"

"Like a baby," Burton answered.

"Are you ready?"

"Yes."

They heard the geese clearly now, calls rising as they approached Cherrygrove. Suddenly they were overhead, swinging down around the depot in a full circle, honking, starting a second circle as they descended in the heavy morning air. Mr. Kraft tapped, "Good-by," and the storks snapped and clicked, "Good-by," and there was really nothing more to say, for the geese were starting their third circle. Mr. Kraft went outside

and watched them, closer than geese had ever come before to Cherrygrove. He heard the storks, then saw them flying upward into the center of the pathfinder V, legs dangling, necks stretched, following the geese out of their last circle, climbing, turning south, geese and storks, arrows against the morning sky, then gone into the soundless sound of time.

✦ ✦ ✦

Through the passing years, the perceptive teachers who came to Cherrygrove were amazed at the knowledge of East Equatorial Africa shown by their students. The children confounded their teachers with bits and pieces of African lore the teachers did not know and could not find in the geography books, the school library, and their own books. How could Cherrygrove sixth graders know that some Kenya cows had red eyes, that sheep wore halters, that traders in the back country had dirty turbans and clean necks, that mail bags were made from a certain material unknown to foreigners. The children spoke of cooking pots and thatched roofs and beds of split bamboo, of white helmets and bare feet, of goats and rubbish heaps, fruit and flame trees, of nights when a police sentry's carbine butt hitting the ground could be heard far away. The children described pigs and chickens, perfumes and stinks, topees and drums and button polish, Bibles and Korans and old London *Times*es. They spoke ever so respectfully of crocodiles and green parakeets, baobabs and mongooses, lions and wild dogs, and the great

breakers of Takaunga Creek that made a sound like a violin string touched by the wind, saying wordlessly that the ship would make Mombasa at dawn.

The teachers said, "How do you know these things?"

"Mr. Kraft told us," said the children.

The teachers called on Mr. Kraft and asked, "How do you know these things?" and Mr. Kraft always replied:

"Oh, the storks told me."

‘ 4 ’

On the day before Christmas in 1935, Mr. Kraft opened the depot for business at the usual time, half an hour before arrival of the eastbound passenger train. He built the fires in the waiting room and office stoves, turned the sounder up on the telegraph, and called "OM - OM - OM." Omaha answered, "ii - ii - OM," and Mr. Kraft sent the figure 5, which meant "Anything for me?" Omaha replied:

"Cablegram for you from Jinja Station, Kenya, Africa, Reads Glad Tidings, signed B and S."

— ..... . — . — ..

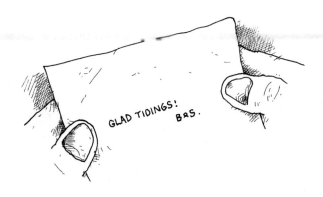